To Mehak
Merry Christmas and Happy New Year

Mr. Tottaran

World of Fairy Tales
The Little Mermaid
and
The Princess and the Pea

Two Tales and Their Histories

alphabet soup™

an imprint of

WINDMILL BOOKS™

New York

Published in 2010 by Windmill Books, LLC
303 Park Avenue South, Suite # 1280, New York, NY 10010-3657

Editor (Arcturus): Carron Brown
Designer: Steve Flight

Library of Congress Cataloging-in-Publication Data

Brown, Carron.
    The little mermaid and The princess and the pea : two tales and their histories / Carron Brown.—
1st North American ed.
        p. cm.— (World of fairy tales)
Summary: A retelling, accompanied by a brief history, of the two well-known tales in the first of which a young mermaid trades her tail for human legs and, in the second, a young girl proves that she is a real princess.
    ISBN 978-1-60754-637-5 (library binding)—ISBN 978-1-60754-638-2 (pbk.)
    ISBN 978-1-60754-639-9 (6-pack)
    1. Fairy tales. [1. Fairy tales.] I. Andersen, H. C. (Hans Christian), 1805–1875. Lille havfrue. II. Andersen, H. C. (Hans Christian), 1805–1875. Prindsessen paa ærten. III. Title. IV. Title: Little mermaid and The princess and the pea. V. Title: Princess and the pea.
    PZ8.B697Lit 2010
    [Fic]—dc22

2009037520

Printed in China

CPSIA Compliance Information: Batch #AW0102W: For further information contact Windmill Books, New York, New York at 1-866-478-0556.

For more great fiction and nonfiction, go to windmillbooks.com.

The Little Mermaid

ONCE UPON A TIME, AT THE BOTTOM OF THE sea, there was a wonderful kingdom of mermaids. On the rocks, many rainbow-colored shellfish opened and shut with the flow of the crystal-clear water, and each one contained a pearl so precious that it would have made the ruler of the richest kingdom turn pale with envy. At the deepest depth stood the King of the Mermaids' castle. The King had six daughters. Each one was beautiful, but the youngest was the fairest of all: her skin was as clear and silky as a rose petal and her eyes were as blue as a lagoon. Sadly, her mother had died soon after the Little Mermaid was born, so she had been brought up by her grandmother, who loved her dearly.

The Little Mermaid was a strange child, quiet and alone.
While her sisters played tirelessly among the seaweed with
fishes and dolphins, she spent her time dreaming.

"Oh," she sighed, "why don't I have legs, so that I could
run on the beach and in the country? Instead, I have this
horrible fish-tail and I must live under water."

Actually, the Little Mermaid was very pretty
with her silver scales, which shone whenever a
sunbeam shimmered down through the water.

One day her grandmother told her:

"When you are fifteen, you can go up to the surface of the sea. You can sit by moonlight on a rock and watch the ships passing."

These words made the Little Mermaid daydream even more. "But I'm only ten. I'll have to wait five long years before I discover the world!"

As the years went by, the Little Mermaid's five sisters all reached their fifteenth birthdays. When they rose together to the surface of the sea before a storm, they swam in front of the ships, singing an enchanting song. Alone in her room, the Little Mermaid awaited her turn. She looked up through the dark blue water and saw the shining stars. And she dreamed; she dreamed of ships, birds, and green hills. At last her birthday arrived. Her beauty was dazzling. Her grandmother crowned her lovely golden curls with white lilies and allowed her to swim up to the surface. Without wasting a moment, the Little Mermaid said good-bye to the sea kingdom and raced upward, higher and higher toward the sky.

Her heart swelled with joy because at last her dream was coming true. The sun had just set when she reached the surface. The clouds were glowing pinky-gold and the evening star was shining down on her. Suddenly she saw a big ship not far off. The Little Mermaid, who was very curious, swam up to the ship's portholes and pulled herself up to look through the glass. Inside, some men were talking, laughing, and singing round a great feast. Among them was a very handsome young prince.

The prince was so handsome that the Little Mermaid felt her heart pounding. She had fallen in love. She stayed for a long time looking through the porthole, wide-eyed with admiration.

Then suddenly she heard a great rumble. The wind rose and the ship began to rock wildly. A terrible storm was brewing. The sea turned black. The panicking sailors ran shouting:

"Furl the sails! Bear to port! Bear to starboard!"

A terrifying lightning flash ripped through the sky, followed by an enormous clap of thunder.

Huge waves crashed onto the ship. Water was pouring into the hold. Suddenly, the Little Mermaid saw the prince. He was drowning and calling desperately for help. She had to save him. She swam to him as fast as she could, grabbed him by the arms, and pulled him up to the surface. Then, gently, she held the prince's head above water and let the waves carry them both onto the beach. There, she fell asleep, tired but happy.

The next morning, the Little Mermaid awoke.
The prince lay beside her, sleeping peacefully. He was
so handsome that she couldn't stop herself from placing a
kiss on his forehead. But the Little Mermaid had to return to
her kingdom. Before she dived, she turned back one last time to
see the prince she loved. It was then that she saw a girl approaching
him. The girl leaned over the prince and softly woke him up.

"He will never know that I saved him," the Little Mermaid
thought sadly. "He will never recognize me."

She let a tear fall and disappeared into the sea. Every night
the Little Mermaid returned to the place where she had left the
prince, and each night she sang of her love for him.

Her voice was so beautiful that all the sea creatures came to
listen to her. But, the prince never heard her. His castle was
too far away and the Little Mermaid could go no further than
the sandy shore. One day she told her grandmother:

"I will give up my mermaid's life to make the prince love me.
Tonight I will go and find the Sea Witch and ask her to give
me legs instead of my fish-tail. Then I will be able to walk
until I find the prince's castle and tell him that it was
I who saved him. And I'll tell him that I love him."

9

Her grandmother tried to stop her, but the Little Mermaid had already made up her mind. The next day she set off for the magic cave where the Sea Witch lived. It was a dark hole at the murky bottom of the sea, where the sun's rays never reached, the silence was deathly and the fish were a sad, gray color. When the Little Mermaid arrived, the Sea Witch said to her:

"I know why you have come. Are you ready to give up your sweet mermaid life for two ridiculous legs?"

The Little Mermaid turned very pale as she replied:

"Yes, I am. I'm in love with a prince and I want to find him in his castle. To do that I need legs, like people have."

At this the Sea Witch heated an enormous cauldron.

"Here is your potion, Little Mermaid," said the witch, and handed her a bottle. "Drink it tomorrow morning at sunrise: your fish-tail will divide and become two legs. Then you can find your prince. But remember: if you are not able to make him love you, on the day that he marries someone else, you will be turned into sea foam."

The Little Mermaid could not imagine something so terrible. How could her prince whom she had saved marry anyone else? So she took the magic potion and began to leave, but the Sea Witch stopped her: "Wait, pretty one. If you want this potion, you'll have to pay me. You have the most beautiful voice in the sea and you must give it to me." The Little Mermaid hesitated, but she loved the prince too much to refuse. So she opened her pretty mouth. Using a sharp blade, the witch cut out her tongue and the Little Mermaid could speak or sing no more. She swam up to the beach and waited for the dawn.

As soon as the sun's first rays appeared, the Little Mermaid opened the bottle, and swallowed its contents in one gulp. Immediately, she fainted with pain and fell down on the sand. As the sun rose higher and its warm rays beamed down on her, the Little Mermaid awoke to find her tail had gone and she had turned into a real girl.

Gradually, she realized a soft sweet voice was speaking. The prince was there, leaning over her. "Who are you?" he asked.

The Little Mermaid wanted to answer, to tell him that it was she who had saved him from drowning and that she loved him. But then she remembered she had lost her tongue.

The prince took the Little Mermaid's hand and led her home to his castle. He offered her magnificent robes and presented her at Court. He called her "my little foundling" and treated her very tenderly, but the idea of marrying her did not enter his head.

"I am fond of you," he told her one day, "because you look like the girl who saved my life after a terrible storm. She found me dying on the beach and soon I am going to marry her, because she is my one true love."

These words made the Little Mermaid's heart ache. She tried to make
the prince understand that it was she who had saved him, but despite
all her efforts, she was unable to say a word. In despair, the Little
Mermaid ran away back to the beach. Days went by. At the castle,
preparations were being made for the prince's wedding. Sitting alone
on a rock by the sea, the Little Mermaid wept for the man she loved.
She knew she could never make him understand and that she had
abandoned her family and lost her wonderful voice all for nothing.

The evening of the wedding arrived. From her rock, the Little Mermaid saw the castle's twinkling lights. The celebrations ended late into the night, when the young bride and groom went to bed. Then the Little Mermaid felt a terrible pain. Her body became light as a feather and broke into a thousand silver stars. She saw many ghostly creatures floating in the air beside her and realized that she had turned into foam as the Sea Witch had foretold.

"We are the daughters of the air," her ghostly friends told her. "Because you have shared the goodness in your heart we welcome you to come with us to the spirit world."

Now that she was invisible, the Little Mermaid flew to the castle and dropped one last kiss on the forehead of the prince she loved. The wind rose and the Little Mermaid was carried off into the sky forever.

THE END

The Princess and the Pea

ONCE UPON A TIME, LONG AGO IN A FARAWAY country, a king and queen lived happily in their splendid palace. Their only son, the prince, was their pride and joy. He was famed for his bravery and good looks and loved to gallop through the woods and fields on his magnificent white horse. All the peasants stopped to watch him pass because they were so proud of their noble prince.

The prince had reached the age to marry and every week, hundreds of marriage proposals arrived at the castle. But the prince did not even open the letters: he preferred riding through the country and talking to the villagers. Nevertheless, when he lay down to rest under the great oaks on the thick soft moss of the forest floor, he would dream of the lady he would marry one day. She would be lovely as the dawn, with long golden hair, sky-blue eyes, and soft skin. She would dance gracefully and be a wonderful musician, she would sing like a bird and her delightful smile would charm the whole kingdom.

She would be a real princess.

One day, the prince was overcome by a deep sadness. He abandoned the forest and its old oaks; his poor horse waited for days for his master to appear. All the people of the kingdom were sad because they no longer saw their handsome prince pass by. Alas, no one could lift him from his gloom: neither his horse's neighing, nor Mary the cook's delicious cakes, nor his gentle mother's pleading.

19

The king and queen were worried by his unhappiness. They begged their son to tell them what was wrong. The prince sighed and told them his secret:

"I am ready to get married, but I want to marry the princess of my dreams. She must be the most beautiful of all princesses. Her eyes must be sky-blue; her skin must be apricot colored. She must be delicate as a flower petal. She must be … a real princess. But I am afraid I will never find her."

"We have to find such a princess," said the queen desperately to her husband. "Only she will be able to cure our son's great sadness."

That very evening, the king called all the young ladies. They came from every kingdom. For seven days and seven nights, the prince saw them one after another: Princess Josephine, Princess Ludivine, Princess Mesallie, Princess Gersande, Princess Eulalie, Princess Ariane… Each time a princess appeared, the prince sadly shook his head. They were all pretty and charming, but each one lacked that little extra something that makes a real princess.

"Since none of these princesses suits you, I'll give you a year to find the woman of your dreams," said the king to his son one day. "If you have not found her by then, you must marry Princess Eleanor, our rich neighbor's daughter."

So the prince spent a year traveling all over the world, riding on his faithful horse. He visited more than a thousand princesses, the daughters of tsars of Russia, emperors of China, maharajahs of India, sheiks of Arabia, American Indian and African chiefs. He met the most beautiful, the most intelligent, the greatest, and the most entertaining young women... But each one lacked that little extra something that makes a real princess.

After three hundred and sixty-five days on his travels, the prince went home disappointed: he had not found his princess. The pleasure of seeing his parents again made him smile for a time, but he soon became sad again. The preparations for his marriage to Eleanor went on in silence. The cooks no longer laughed in the kitchens, the jugglers no longer played in the courtyards, the peasants no longer sang in the fields. The whole kingdom was affected by its prince's sadness.

21

One night,
there was a
terrible storm:
an icy wind blew
through the castle's
towers, the ground shook
at each crack of thunder,
and terrifying flashes of
lightning lit up the sky.

Suddenly, there was a knock on the heavy palace door. The old king was astounded that anyone should be out on such a night and went to open the door himself. On the doorstep he found a young woman, who was wet through and shivering with cold and fear.

"Come in and get warm, my poor child," the king said to her, "and tell us what has happened to you."

"Sire, my name is Inez. I am a princess, Princess Inez. The storm overturned my carriage and the thunder frightened my servants away. I have come to ask you for your hospitality, Sire."

Although she was very pretty, the young woman was in a sorry state: her clothes were torn and her hair all tangled.

She doesn't look at all like a
princess, thought the queen. Perhaps
this young woman is telling us stories.
I have an idea ... an idea that will
let me know the truth.

And without saying a word,
the queen went off to prepare a
bedroom for her guest, muttering:

"A princess? Well, we'll see
about that!"

The queen stripped the bed and put a tiny little pea on one of the slats—a tiny little pea that was green and round—and on top of that she placed twenty mattresses. Then she put twenty blankets on top of those twenty mattresses.

"I have made you the most comfortable bed in the whole palace," she said to Princess Inez. "I hope you will sleep well."

She helped the princess step onto the first rung of the ladder up into her bed.

The next morning, the sun came out again and shone down on the
kingdom. Inez sat down to a mighty breakfast. Then the queen asked her
guest if she had had a good night's sleep. The prince, who was aware of the
trap the queen had set in order to discover whether she was a real princess,
waited impatiently for the young woman's answer. Had she slept well?

"I have never slept worse in all my life," Inez replied, shyly. "Forgive my
rudeness, but there was something in my bed, something horribly hard,
which stopped me from getting a wink of sleep. I am stiff all over."

The embarrassed princess lifted the hem of her dress and showed the astonished prince two charming ankles covered in bruises. When she saw this, the queen hugged her son and then the king kissed him at least ten times. They laughed and cried, while the prince kept on repeating in amazement:

"I've found her! I've found her!"

At last he had found his real princess: only a real princess would have been so delicate as to feel a tiny, round green pea through twenty mattresses and twenty blankets!

The charming prince won the beautiful Princess Inez's heart at once. He presented her to the people of his kingdom, showed her around the palace, and took her to the forest. Inez delighted all who saw her with her beauty and kindness, and the king and queen loved her dearly. The kingdom smiled again and, in this happy, joyful atmosphere, the prince married the woman he had always dreamed of. They lived happily ever after and had lots of real little princes and real little princesses.

The queen picked out the pea and had it displayed on a velvet cushion in the kingdom's museum, where it can still be seen to this day.

THE END

History of The Little Mermaid

This fairy tale was written by the Danish author Hans Christian Andersen in 1836. It was translated into English in 1872. Unlike most other fairy tales, this one is not based on any previous story—Hans Christian Andersen is the first author of the tale.

However, the author would have heard about mermaids from the stories that he was told as a child. The fairy tale collection called *The Arabian Nights*, which Hans Christian Andersen read when he was growing up, contains stories featuring sea people. Mermaids are mythological creatures, and stories about them have been told for thousands of years all over the world. The beautiful songs of mermaids were said to enchant sailors and draw them close to the rocks during storms. It is now thought that the haunting sounds that sailors heard were probably made by sea mammals, such as seals.

The first stories known about mermaids come from Assyria (modern-day Iraq) and date from 1000 BCE. They feature a goddess queen who dives into a river to stop people from noticing how beautiful she is, but the water cannot hide her beauty. So she becomes a mermaid. In the earliest pictures that accompany this tale, the queen is shown as a fish's body with a human head and legs. The mermaid body that we know now—a fish-tail and a human's upper body—has been created over many centuries of storytelling.

Since then, mermaids have appeared in many tales. In some, they are good and kind, like the Little Mermaid, helping sailors survive the terrifying seas. In other stories, mermaids have caused the death of sailors and are seen as signs of doom. They were even said to swim up rivers to lakes.

The "Little Mermaid" has been made into several films, with the most recent made in 1989 by Walt Disney. A statue of the Little Mermaid can be seen on a rock in Copenhagen Harbor, Denmark.

History of The Princess and the Pea

"The Princess and the Pea" is a fairy tale by the Danish author Hans Christian Andersen and was first published in 1835 in a booklet called *Fairy Tales Told for Children*. The author was told many stories when he was growing up and these fired his imagination. It is likely that "The Princess and the Pea" is one of the tales that was passed from person to person, rather than the author reading it from a book. Unfortunately, its original source is lost to history.

Similar tales of "The Princess and the Pea" tell of a lady who isn't a real princess learning about the pea test from a friend. The lady then tricks the royal family into thinking that she felt the pea through the mattress and so they believe she is a true princess. Hans Christian Andersen made the princess in his story truly feel the pea and have a bad night's sleep, so she is not a trickster but a real princess.

Hans Christian Andersen wrote of some his stories for children, which was very unusual as most of the fairy tale writers of the early 19th century wrote the stories for adults to read. The people who reviewed the books Hans Christian Andersen wrote didn't like them because the chatty language he used was for younger readers, and he added features to the story that would make his readers smile, such as the pea being in the king's museum. In translations of the story at the time, this fun ending was often taken out because the translator didn't think it was a serious end to the tale.

The moral of "The Princess and the Pea" is not to go by first appearances. The queen didn't think the girl was a true princess because she was bedraggled when she arrived at the castle. It is only when the princess passes the pea test that the queen realizes that the girl was a princess all the time.

In the past century, the story has gained in popularity, and been made into television programs, musical theater productions, movies, books, and short stories.